Percy B. Shelley

Letters from Percy Bysshe Shelley to William Godwin

Volume 1

Percy B. Shelley

Letters from Percy Bysshe Shelley to William Godwin
Volume 1

ISBN/EAN: 9783337388065

Printed in Europe, USA, Canada, Australia, Japan

Cover: Foto ©Andreas Hilbeck / pixelio.de

More available books at **www.hansebooks.com**

LETTERS

FROM

PERCY BYSSHE SHELLEY

TO

WILLIAM GODWIN.

IN TWO VOLUMES.

VOL. I.

1891.
London : Privately Printed.
(Not for Sale.)

CONTENTS.

VOL. I.

VOL. I. *b*

CONTENTS.

CONTENTS.

PAGE

LETTERS.

B

LETTERS TO
WILLIAM GODWIN.

LETTER I.

KESWICK, CUMBERLAND.
January 3rd, 1812.
[*Friday*].

SIR,

You will be surprised at hearing
from a stranger. No introduction has,
nor in all probability ever will, authorize
that which common thinkers would call
a liberty. It is however a liberty which,
although not sanctioned by custom, is
so far from being reprobated by reason

that the dearest interests of mankind imperiously demand that a certain etiquette of fashion should no longer keep "man at a distance from man," or impose its flimsy fancies between the free communication of intellect.

The name of Godwin has been used to excite in me feelings of reverence and admiration. I have been accustomed to consider him a luminary too dazzling for the darkness which surrounds him. From the earliest period of my knowledge of his principles, I have ardently desired to share, on the footing of intimacy, that intellect which I have delighted to contemplate in its emanations.

Considering, then, these feelings, you will not be surprised at the inconceivable emotions with which I learned your existence and your dwelling. I had enrolled your name in the list of the honourable dead. I had felt regret that the glory of your being had passed from this earth of ours. It is not so; you still live, and, I firmly believe, are still planning the welfare of human kind.

I have but just entered on the scene of human operations; yet my feelings and my reasonings correspond with what yours were. My course has been short, but eventful. I have seen much of human prejudice, suffered much from human persecution, yet I see no reason hence inferrible which should alter my wishes for their renovation. The ill-treatment I have met with has more than ever impressed the truth of my principles on my judgment. I am young, I am ardent in the cause of philanthropy and truth. Do not suppose that this is vanity; I am not conscious that it influences this portraiture. I imagine myself dispassionately describing the state of my mind. I am young; you have gone before me,—I doubt not, are a veteran to me in the years of persecution. Is it strange that, defying prejudice as I have done, I should outstep the limits of custom's prescription, and endeavour to make my desire useful by a friendship with William Godwin ?

I pray you to answer this letter. Imperfect as may be my capacity, my desire is ardent and unintermitted. Half an hour would be at least humanely employed in the experiment. I may mistake your residence ; certain feelings, of which I may be an inadequate arbiter, may induce you to desire concealment; I may not, in fine, have an answer to this letter. If I do not, when I come to London I shall seek for you. I am convinced I could represent myself to you in such terms as not to be thought wholly unworthy of your friendship; at least, if desire for universal happiness has any claim upon your preference, that desire I can exhibit.

Adieu.   I shall earnestly await your answer.

PERCY B. SHELLEY.

To
   Mr. William Godwin,
     at M. J. Godwin's Juvenile Library,
       Skinner Street,
         London.

LETTER II.

KESWICK, [CUMBERLAND.]
January 10*th*, 1812.
[*Friday*].

SIR,

It is not otherwise to be supposed than that I should appreciate your avocations far beyond the pleasure or benefit which can accrue to me from their sacrifice. The time, however, will be small which may be mis-spent in reading this letter; and, much individual pleasure as an answer might give me, I have not the vanity to imagine that it will be greater than the happiness elsewhere diffused during the time which its creation will occupy.

You complain that the generalizing character of my letter renders it deficient in interest; that I am not an individual to you. Yet, intimate as I am with your character and your writings, intimacy with *yourself* must in some degree precede this exposure of my peculiarities. It is scarcely possible, however pure be the morality which he has endeavoured to diffuse, but that generalization must characterize the uninvited address of a stranger to a stranger.

I proceed to remedy the fault. I am the son of a man of fortune in Sussex. The habits of thinking of my father and myself never coincided. Passive obedience was inculcated and enforced in my childhood. I was required to love, because it was *my duty* to love : it is scarcely necessary to remark that coercion obviated its own intention. I was haunted with a passion for the wildest and most extravagant romances. Ancient books of Chemistry and Magic were perused with an enthusiasm of wonder, almost amounting to belief. My sentiments were unrestrained by anything within me ; external impediments were numerous, and strongly applied ; their effect was merely temporary.

From a reader, I became a writer, of romances ; before the age of seventeen * I had published two, *St. Irvyne* and *Zastrozzi*, each of which, though quite uncharacteristic of me as now I am, yet serves to mark the state of my mind at the period of their composition. I shall desire them to be sent to you : do not, however, consider this as any obligation to yourself to misapply your valuable time.

* Shelley is incorrect in stating that he had published two novels "before the age of seventeen." Shelley was born on *August 4th*, 1792, and as *Zastrozzi* was published on *June 5th*, 1810 [D. F. MacCarthy : *Shelley's Early Life*, 1872. p. 12]. he was just seventeen years and ten months old at the date of its issue. *St. Irvyne* was published on or about *December 20th*, 1810, at which date Shelley was fully eighteen years and four months old. This is not the only instance in which he understated his age ; possibly through negligence of mind, or possibly (suggests Mr. Rossetti) with a spice of coxcombry.

It is now a period of more than two years since first I saw your inestimable book of *Political Justice*.   It opened to my mind fresh and more extensive views ;   it materially influenced my character, and I rose from its perusal a wiser and a better man.   I was no longer the votary of romance ;   till then I had existed in an ideal world—now I found that in this universe of ours was enough to excite the interest of the heart, enough to employ the discussions of reason ;   I beheld, in short, that I had duties to perform.   Conceive the effect which the *Political Justice* would have upon a mind before jealous of its independence, participating somewhat singularly in a peculiar susceptibility.

My age is now *nineteen;* at the period to which I allude I was at Eton.   No sooner had I formed the principles which I now profess than I was anxious to disseminate their benefits.   This was done without the slightest caution.   I was twice expelled, but recalled by the interference of my father. I went to Oxford. Oxonian society was insipid to me, uncongenial with my habits of thinking. I could not descend to common life : the sublime interest of poetry, lofty and exalted achievements, the proselytism of the world, the equalization of its inhabitants, were to me the soul of my soul. You can probably form some idea of the con‑ trast exhibited to my character by those with whom I was surrounded. Classical reading and poetical writing employed me during my residence at Oxford.

In the meantime I became, in the popular sense of the word, a sceptic. I printed a pamphlet, avowing my opinion, and its occasion. I distributed this anonymously to men of thought and learning, wishing that Reason should decide on the case at issue ; it was never my intention to deny it.

Mr. ——, at Oxford, among others, had the pamphlet ; he showed it to the Master and the Fellows of University College, and I was sent for. I was informed that, in case I denied the publication, no more would be said. I refused, and was expelled.

It will be necessary, in order to elucidate this part of my history, to inform you that I am heir by entail to an estate of £6000 per annum. My principles have induced me to regard the law of primogeniture as an evil of primary magnitude. My father's notions of family honour are incoincident with my knowledge of public good. I will never sacrifice the latter to any consideration. My father has ever regarded me as a blot, a defilement of his honour. He wished to induce me by poverty to accept of some commission in a distant regiment ; and, in the interim of my absence, to prosecute the pamphlet, that a process of outlawry might make the estate, on his death, devolve to my younger brother.

These are the leading points of the history of the man before you. Others exist, but I have thought proper to make some selection, not that it is my design to conceal or extenuate any part, but that I should by their enumeration quite outstep the bounds of modesty. Now, it is for you to judge whether, by permitting me to cultivate your friendship, you are exhibiting yourself more really useful than by the pursuance of those avocations of which the time spent in allowing this cultivation would deprive you. I am now earnestly pursuing studious habits. I am writing "An enquiry into the causes of the failure of the French Revolution to benefit mankind." My plan is that of resolving to lose no opportunity to disseminate truth and happiness.

I am married to a woman whose views are similar to my own. To you, as the regulator and former of my mind, I must ever look with real respect and veneration.

Yours sincerely,

P. B. SHELLEY,

To

 Mr. William Godwin,

    London.

LETTER III.

KESWICK, [CUMBERLAND].
January 16th, 1812.
[*Thursday.*]

MY DEAR SIR,

That so prompt and so kind an answer should have relieved my mind I had scarcely dared to hope. To find that he—who as an author had gained my love and confidence, whose views and habits I had delighted to conjecture from his works, whose principles I had adopted, and every trace of whose existence is now made sacred, and I hope eternally so, by associations which throw the charm of feeling over the deductions of reason—that he, as a man, should be my friend and my adviser, the moderator of my enthusiasm, the personal exciter and strengthener of my virtuous habits: all this was more than I dared to trust myself to hope, and which now comes to me almost like a ray of second existence.

Without the deceit of self-flattery, which might lead me to think that my intellectual powers demanded your time, those circumstances, which arbitrarily—or, as may be said, fortuitously—place me in a situation capable hereafter of considerably influencing the actions of others, induce me to think I shall not

> " In publica commoda peccem,
> Si longo sermone morer tua tempora."

I know not how to describe the pleasure which your last letter has given me; that William Godwin should have " a deep and earnest interest in *my* welfare," cannot but produce the most intoxicating sensations.   It may be my vanity which is thus flattered; but I am much deceived in myself, if love and respect for the great and worthy form not a very considerable part of my feelings.

I cannot help considering you as a friend and adviser whom I have known very long; this circumstance must generate a degree of familiarity, which will cease to appear surprising to you, when [it is considered that] the intimacy which I had acquired with your writings so much preceded the information which led to my first letter.

It may be said that I have derived little benefit or injury from artificial education.   I have known no tutor or adviser (*not excepting my father*) from whose lessons and suggestions I have not recoiled with disgust.

The knowledge which I have, whatever it may be (putting out of the
question the age of the grammar and
the horn-book) has been acquired by
my unassisted efforts. I have before
given you a slight sketch of my earlier
habits and feelings. My present are,
in my own opinion, infinitely superior
—they are elevated and disinterested :
such as they are, *you* have principally.
produced them.

With what delight, what cheerful-
ness, what good will, may it be conceived that I constitute myself the
pupil of him, under whose actual
guidance my very thoughts have hitherto been arranged !

You mistake me if you think that I
am angry with my father. I have ever
been desirous of a reconciliation with
him ; but the price which he demands
for it is a renunciation of my opinions,
or, at least, a subjection to conditions
which should bind me to act in oppo-

sition to their very spirit. It is probable that my father has *acted* for my
welfare, but the manner in which he
has done so will not allow me to
suppose that he has *felt* for it, uncon-
nectedly with certain considerations of
birth ; and feeling for these things was
not feeling for me. I never loved my
father :—it was not from hardness of
heart, for I have loved and do love
warmly.

You say, " Being yet a scholar, I
ought to have no intolerable itch to
become a teacher." I have not,—so
far as any publications of mine are
irreconcilable with the general good, or
so far as they are negative. I do not
set up for a judge of controversies ;
but, into whatever company I go, I
have introduced my own sentiments,—
partly with a view, if they were any
wise erroneous, that unforeseen eluci-
dations might rectify them ; or, if they
were not, that I should contribute my

mite to the treasury of wisdom and happiness.

I hope in the course of our communication to acquire that sobriety of spirit which is the characteristic of true heroism.

I have not heard without benefit that Newton was a modest man : I am not ignorant that vanity and folly delight in forwardness and assumption. But I think there is a line to be drawn between affectation of unpossessed talents, and the deceit of self-distrust, by which much power has been lost to the world ; for

" Full many a flower is born to blush unseen,
And waste its sweetness on the desert air."

This line may be called " the modesty of nature." I hope I am somewhat anxious not to outstep its boundaries. I will not again crudely obtrude the question of atheism on the world. But could I not at the same time improve my own powers, and diffuse true and virtuous principles? Many, with equally confined talents to my own, are by publications scattering the seeds of prejudice and selfishness. Might not an exhibition of truth, with equal elegance and depth, suffice to counteract the deleterious tendency of their principles? Does not writing hold the next place to colloquial discussion in eliciting and classing the powers of the mind?* I am willing to become a scholar—nay, a pupil. My humility and confidence, where I am conscious that I am not imposed upon, and where I perceive talents and powers so certainly and undoubtedly superior, is unfeigned and complete.

I have desired the publications of my early youth to be sent to you. You will perceive that *Zastrozzi* and *St. Irvyne* were written prior to my ac-

* This is in conformity with Godwin's own propositions in his *Political Justice*.

quaintance with your writings; the *Essay on Love*, a little poem, since. I had, indeed, read *St. Leon* before I wrote *St. Irvyne*; but the reasonings had *then* made little impression.

In a few days we set off to Dublin. I do not know exactly where we shall be; but a letter addressed to Keswick will find me. Our journey has been settled some time. We go principally to *forward as much as we can* the Catholic Emancipation.

Southey the poet, whose principles were pure and elevated once, is now the paid champion of every abuse and absurdity. I have had much conversation with him. He says, "You will think as I do when you are as old." I do not feel the least disposition to be Mr. S[outhey]'s proselyte.

In the summer we shall be in the north of Wales. Dare I hope that you will come to see us? Perhaps this is an unfeasible neglect of your avocations.   I shall hope it until you forbid me.

I remain, with the greatest respect,
Your most sincere and devoted
PERCY B. SHELLEY.

To
  Mr. William Godwin,
London.

LETTER IV.

KESWICK, CUMBERLAND.
January 28th, 1812.
[*Tuesday.*]

MY DEAR SIR,

Your letter has reached me on the eve of our departure for Dublin. I cannot deny myself the pleasure of answering it, although we shall probably have reached Ireland before an answer to this can arrive. You do us a great and essential service by the enclosed introduction to Mr. Curran; he is a man whose public character I have admired and respected. You offer an additional motive for hastening our journey.

I have not long been married. My wife is the partner of my thoughts and feelings. *My* state, at the period of our first knowledge of each other, was isolated and friendless; *hers* was embittered by family disagreements, and a system of domestic oppressions. We agreed to unite our fates; and the reasons that operated to induce our submission to the ceremonies of the Church were the many advantages of benefiting society which the despotism of custom would cut us off from in case of our nonconformity. My peculiar reasons were considerations of the unequally weighty burden of disgrace and hatred which a resistance to this system would entail upon my companion. A man in such a case is a man of gallantry and spirit—a woman loses all claim to respect and politeness. She has lost modesty, which is the female criterion of virtue, and those whose virtues extend no farther than modesty regard her with hatred and contempt.

You regard early authorship [as] detrimental to the cause of general happiness. I confess this has not been my opinion, even when I have bestowed deep, and I hope disinterested, thought upon the subject.

If any man would determine, sincerely and cautiously, at *every* period of his life, to publish books which should contain the real state of his feelings and opinions, I am willing to suppose that this portraiture of his mind would be worth many metaphysical disquisitions ; and one, whose mind is strongly imbued with an ardent desire of communicating pleasurable sensations is of all others the least likely to publish any feelings or opinions but such as should excite the reader to discipline in some sort his mind into the same state as that of the writer.

With these sentiments I have been preparing an Address to the Catholics

of Ireland, which, however deficient
may be its execution, I can by no
means admit that it contains one
sentiment which *can* harm the cause of
liberty and happiness. It consists of
the benevolent and tolerant deductions
of philosophy reduced into the sim-
plest language, and such as those who
by their uneducated poverty are most
susceptible of evil impressions from
Catholicism may clearly comprehend.
I know it can do no harm ; it cannot
excite rebellion, as its main principle
is to trust the success of a cause to the
energy of its truth. It cannot " widen
the breach between the kingdoms," as
it attempts to convey to the vulgar
mind sentiments of universal philanthropy ; and, whatever impressions it
may produce, they can be no others
but those of peace and harmony. It
owns no religion but benevolence, no
cause but virtue, no party but the
world. I shall devote myself with un-

remitting zeal, as far as an uncertain state of health will permit, towards forwarding the great ends of virtue and happiness in Ireland, regarding as I do the present state of that country's affairs as an opportunity which if I, being thus disengaged, permit to pass unoccupied, I am unworthy of the character which I have assumed.— Enough of Ireland.

I anticipated in my own mind your sentiments on the remark which you quoted from my last letter concerning my father. I am not a stranger to the immense complexity of human feelings; but, when I find generosity so exceedingly outweighed in any one's conduct by the contrary and less extended principle, then I despair of good fruits, seeing marks of barrenness. I have a great wish of adding to my father's happiness, because the filial connection seems to render it, as it were, more particularly in my power;

but it is impossible. A little while since he sent to me a letter, through his attorney, renewing an allowance of two hundred pounds per annum, but with the remark "that his sole reason for so doing was to prevent my cheating strangers." The insult contained in these words, as applied to me, excites no feeling of repulsion or hatred towards him, but it makes me despair of conciliation, when I see how rooted is his prejudice against me.

I find myself near the end of my paper. My egotism appears inexhaustible. My relation of pupilage with regard to you in a manner excuses this apparent vanity. I wish to put you in possession of as much of my thoughts and feelings as I know myself. I shall regard as a most inestimable blessing my happy audacity in casting aside the trammels of custom, and drinking the streams of your mind at their fountain-head.

I will say no more of Wales at present. We have determined, next summer, to receive a most dear friend,* of whom I shall speak hereafter, in some romantic spot. Perhaps I shall be able to prevail on you, and your wife and children, to leave the tumult and dust of London for a while. However that may be, I shall certainly see you in London. I am not yet of age. At that time I have great hopes of being enabled to offer you a house of my own. Philanthropy is confined to no spot.—Adieu !

Direct your next " Post Office, Dublin." My wife sends her respects.

Believe me, in all sincerity of heart,
Yours truly, sincerely,
P. B. SHELLEY.

To
Mr. William Godwin,
London.

* Miss Elizabeth Hitchener.

LETTER V.

[7, LOWER SACKVILLE STREET],
DUBLIN.
February 24th, 1812.
[*Monday.*]

MY DEAR SIR,

A most tedious journey by sea and land has brought us to our destination. I have delayed a few days informing you of it, because I enclose with this a little pamphlet which I have just printed, and thereby save a double expense. I have wilfully vulgarized the language of this pamphlet, in order to reduce the remarks it contains to the taste and comprehension of the Irish peasantry, who have been too long brutalized by vice and ignorance. I conceive that the benevolent passions of their breasts are in some degree excited, and individual interests in some degree generalized, by Catholic disqualifications and the oppressive influence of the Union Act ; that some degree of indignation has arisen at the conduct of the Prince Regent, which might tend to blind insurrections. A crisis like this ought not to be permitted to pass unoccupied or unimproved.

I have another pamphlet in the press, earnestly recommending to a different class the institution of a philanthropic society. No *unnatural unanimity* can take place, if secessions of the minority on any question are invariably made. It might segregate into twenty different societies, each coinciding generically, though differing specifically.

We have had a most tedious voyage. We were driven by a storm completely to the north of Ireland, in our passage from the Isle of Man. Harriet my wife, and Eliza my sister-in-law, were very much fatigued, after twenty-eight hours' tossing in a galliot during a violent gale. They are now tolerably recovered.

I am exceedingly obliged by your letter of introduction to Mr. Curran. His speeches had interested me before I had any idea of coming to Ireland. It seems that he was the only man who would engage in behalf of the prisoners during the times of horror of the Rebellions. I have called upon him twice, but have not found him at home.

I hope that the motives which induce me to publish thus early in life do not arise from any desire of distinguishing myself any more than is consistent with, and subordinate to, usefulness. In the first place, my physical constitution is such as will not permit me to hope for a life so long as yours ;—the person who is constitutionally nervous, and affected by slight fatigue at the age of nineteen, cannot expect firmness and health at fifty. I have therefore resolved to husband whatever powers I may possess, so that they may turn to the best account. I find that whilst my mind is actively engaged in writing or discussion, it gains strength at the same time,—that the results of its present power are incorporated. I find that subjects grow out of conversation, and that, though I begin a subject in writing with no definite view, it presently assumes a definite form, in consequence of the method that grows out of the induced train of thought. I therefore write ; and I publish, because I will publish nothing that shall not conduce to virtue, and therefore my publications, so far as they do influence, shall influence to good. My views of society, and my hopes of it, meet with congenial ones in few breasts. But virtue and truth are congenial to many. I will employ no means but these for my object; and, however visionary some may regard the ultimatum that I propose, if they act virtuously they will, equally with myself, forward its accomplishment. And my publications will present to the moralist and metaphysician a picture of a mind, however juvenile and unformed, which had, at the dawn of its knowledge, taken a singular turn; and to leave out the early lineaments of its appearance would be to efface those which the attrition of the world had not deprived of right-angled originality.—Thus much for egotism.

I am sorry that you cannot come to Wales in the summer. I had pictured to my fancy that I should first meet you in a spot like that in which Fleetwood met Ruffigny; that then every lesson of your wisdom might become associated in my mind with the forms of Nature where she sports in the simplicity of her loveliness and magnificence, and each become imperishable together. This must not be yet. I will, however, hope that at some future time the sunset of your evening days may irradiate my soul, in scenes like these. I will come to London next autumn. A very dear friend has promised to visit us in Merionethshire in the summer ; and I will own that I am not sufficient of a Stoic not to perceive that the grand and ravishing shapes of Nature add to the joys of friendship. Besides, you must know that I either am or fancy myself something of a poet.

You speak of my wife. She desires, with me, to you, and to all connected with you, her best regards. She is a woman whose pursuits, hopes, fears, and sorrows, were so similar to my own that we married a few months ago. I hope in the course of this year to introducè her to you and yours, as I have introduced myself to you. It is only to those who have had some share in making me what I am that I can be thus free.—Adieu.

You will hear from me shortly. Give my love and respects to every one with whom you are connected. I feel myself almost at your fire-side.

Yours very sincerely,

P. B. SHELLEY.

Have they sent you the books? I send the little book for which I was expelled. I know that Milton believed Christianity, but I do not forget that Virgil believed ancient mythology.

To
  Mr. W. Godwin,
    London.

LETTER VI.

[7, Lower] SACKVILLE STREET,
DUBLIN.
March 8th, 1812.
[*Sunday.*]

MY DEAR SIR,

Your letter affords me much food for thought; guide thou and direct me. In all the weakness of my inconsistencies, bear with me. The genuine respect which I bear for your character, the love with which your virtues have inspired me, is undiminished by any suspicion of externally-constituted authority; when *you* reprove me, Reason speaks; I acquiesce in her decisions. I know that I am vain; that I assume a character which is perhaps unadapted to the limitedness of my experience;

that I am without the modesty which is so generally considered an indispensable ornament to the ingenuousness of youth. I attempt not to conceal from others, or myself, these deficiencies, if such they are. That I have erred in pursuance of this line of conduct, I am well aware : in the opposite case, I think that my errors would have been more momentous and overwhelming. "A preponderance of resulting good is imagined in every action." I certainly believe that the line of conduct which I am now pursuing will produce a preponderance of good ; when I get rid of this conviction, my conduct shall be changed.

Enquiry is doubtless necessary,— nay, essential. I am eagerly open to every new information. I attempt to read a book which attacks my most cherished sentiments, as calmly as one which corroborates them. I have *not* "read your writings slightly." They have made a deep impression on my mind; their arguments are fresh in my memory; I have daily occasion to recur to them; as allies in the cause which I am here engaged in vindicating. To them, to you, I owe the inestimable boon of granted power, of arising from the state of intellectual sickliness and lethargy into which I was plunged two years ago, and of which *St. Irvyne* and *Zastrozzi* were the distempered although unoriginal visions.

I am not forgetful or unheeding of what you said of associations. But *Political Justice* was first published in 1793; nearly twenty years have elapsed since the general diffusion of its doctrines. What has followed? Have men ceased to fight? Have vice and misery vanished from the earth? Have the fire-side communications which it recommends taken place? Out of the many who have read that inestimable book, how many have been blinded by prejudice! How many, in short, have taken it up to gratify an ephemeral vanity; and, when the hour of its novelty had passed, threw it aside, and yielded, with fashion, to the arguments of Mr. Malthus!

I have at length proposed a Philanthropic Association, which I conceive not to be contradictory, but strictly compatible with the principles of *Political Justice.* The *Address* was principally designed to operate on the Irish Mob. Can they be in a worse state than at present? Intemperance and hard labour have reduced them to machines. The oyster that is washed and driven at the mercy of the tides appears to me an animal of almost equal elevation in the scale of intellectual being. Is it impossible to awaken a moral sense in the breasts of those who appear so unfitted for the high destination of their nature? Might not an unadorned display of moral truth, suited to their

comprehensions, produce the best ef-
fects? The state of Society appears to
me to be retrogressive. If there be any
truth in the hopes which I so fondly
cherish, then this cannot be. Yet, even
if it be stationary, the eager activity of
philanthropists is demanded. I think
of the last twenty years with impatient
scepticism as to the progress which the
human mind has made during this
period. I will own that I am eager
that something should be done. But
my Association. In some Suggestions *
respecting it, I have the following :—

"That any number of persons who
meet together for philanthropical purposes should ascertain by friendly discussion those points of opinion wherein
they differ, and those wherein they co-
incide ; and should, by subjecting them
to rational analysis, produce an unani-

---

* Apparently Shelley had written out a paper of
Suggestions intended to follow the *Proposals for an
Association*, &c. Nothing further is known of the
Suggestions.

mity founded on reason, and not the superficial agreement too often exhibited at associations for mere party purposes ;—that the minority, whose belief could not subscribe to the opinion of the majority on a division in any question of moment and interest, should secede. . . . . Some associations might, by refinement of secessions, contain not more than three or four members."

I do not think a society such as this is incompatible with your chapter on associations; it purposes no violent or immediate measures ; its intentions are a facilitation of enquiry, and actually to carry into effect those confidential and private communications which you recommend. I send you with this the *Proposals,* which will be followed by the *Suggestions.*

I had no conception of the depth of human misery until now. The poor of Dublin are assuredly the meanest and most miserable of all. In their narrow streets thousands seem huddled together,—one mass of animated filth. With what eagerness do such scenes as these inspire me! How self-confident, too, do I feel in my assumption to teach the lessons of virtue to those who grind their fellow beings into worse than annihilation! These were the persons to whom, in my fancy, I had addressed myself. How quickly were my views on this subject changed! Yet how deeply has this very change rooted the conviction on which I came hither.

I do not think that my book can in the slightest degree tend to violence. The pains which I have taken, even to tautology, to insist on pacific measures,—the necessity which every warrior and rebel must lie under to deny almost every passage of my book, before he can become so—must at least exculpate me from tending to make him so.

I shudder to think that for the very

roof that covers me, for the bed whereon
I lie, I am indebted to the selfishness
of man.   A remedy must somewhere
have a beginning.   Have I explained
myself clearly?   Are we now at issue?

I have not seen Mr. Curran.   I have
called repeatedly, left my address and
my pamphlet.   I *will* see him before I
leave Dublin.

I send a newspaper and the *Proposals*.   I had no conception that the
packet I sent you would be sent by
the post; I thought it would have
reached you per coach.

Harriet joins in respects to you.   Is
your denial respecting Wales irrevoc-
able?   Would not your children gain
health and spirits from the jaunt?

With sincerest respect yours,

P. B. SHELLEY.

You will see the account of ME in
the newspaper.   I am vain, but not so
foolish as not to be rather piqued than

gratified at the eulogia of a journal. I
have repeated my injunctions concerning *St. I[rvyne]* and *Z[astrozzi]*.

"Expenditure" is used in my *Address* in a moral sense.

To
  Mr. William Godwin.
        London.

LETTER VII.

17, GRAFTON STREET,
[DUBLIN].
March 18*th*, 1812.
[*Wednesday.*]

MY DEAR SIR,

I have said that I acquiesce in your decision, nor has my conduct militated with the assertion. I have withdrawn from circulation the publications wherein I erred, and am preparing to quit Dublin. It is not because I think that *such* associations as I conceived would be deleterious that I have withdrawn them. It is possible to festinate, or retard, the progress of human perfectibility. Such associations as I would have recommended would be calculated to produce the former effect; the refinement of secessions would prevent a fictitious unanimity; as their publicity would render ineffectual any schemes of violent innovation. I am not one of those whom pride will restrain from admitting my own short-sightedness, or confessing a conviction which wars with those previously avowed. My schemes of organizing the ignorant I confess to be ill-timed. I cannot conceive that they were dangerous, as unqualified publicity was likewise enforced; moreover, I do not see that a peasant would attentively read my address, and, arising from the perusal, become imbued in sentiments of violence and bloodshed.

It is indescribably painful to contemplate beings capable of soaring to the heights of science, with Newton and Locke, without attempting to awaken them from a state of lethargy so opposite. The part of this city called the Liberty exhibits a spectacle of

squalidness and misery such as might
reasonably excite impatience in a cooler
temperament than mine. But I submit; I shall address myself no more to
the illiterate. I will look to events in
which it will be impossible that I can
share, and make myself the cause of
an effect which will take place ages
after I have mouldered in the dust; I
need not observe that this resolve requires stoicism. To return to the
heartless bustle of ordinary life, to take
interest in its uninteresting details, I
cannot. Wholly to abstract our views
from self undoubtedly requires unpar-
alleled disinterestedness. There is not
a completer abstraction than labouring
for distant ages.

My Association scheme undoubtedly
grew out of my notions of "political
justice," first generated by your book
on that subject. I had not, however,
read in vain of confidential discussions,
and a recommendation for their gene-

ral adoption; not in vain had I been warned against a fictitious [qy. *facti-tious*] unanimity. I have had the opportunity of witnessing the latter at public dinners. The peculiarity of my Association would have consisted in combining the adoption of the former with the rejection of the latter. Moreover, I desired to sink the question of immediate grievance in the more general and remote consideration of a highly perfectible state of society. I desired to embrace the present opportunity for attempting to forward the accomplishment of that event, and my ultimate views looked to an establishment of those familiar parties for discussion which have not yet become general.

It appears to me that on the publication of *Political Justice* you looked to a more rapid improvement than has taken place. It is my opinion that, if your book had been as general as the Bible, human affairs would now have exhibited a very different aspect.

I have read your letters,—read them with the attention and reverence they deserve. Had *I*, like you, been witness to the French Revolution, it is probable that my caution would have been greater. I have seen and heard enough to make me doubt the omnipotence of truth in a society so constituted as that wherein we live. I shall make you acquainted with all my proceedings; if I err, probe me severely.

If I was alone, and had made no engagements, I would immediately come to London: as it is, I defer it for a time. We leave Dublin in three weeks.

A woman of extraordinary talents,* whom I am so happy as to enroll in the list of those who esteem me, has engaged to visit me in Wales. Mrs. Shelley earnestly desires me to make

* Miss Elizabeth Hitchener.

one last attempt to induce you to visit Wales. If *you* absolutely cannot, may not your amiable family, with whom we all long to become acquainted, breathe with us the pure air of the mountains? Lest there be any informality in the petition, Mrs. Shelley desires her regards to Mrs. Godwin and family, urging the above. Miss Westbrook, my sister-in-law, resides with us; and in one thing, at least, none of us are deficient, viz., zeal and sincerity.

Fear no more for any violence or hurtful measures in which I may be instrumental in Dublin. My mind is now by no means settled on the subject of Associations: they appear to me in one point of view useful, in another deleterious. I acquiesce in your decisions. I am neither haughty, reserved, nor unpersuadable. I hope that time will show your pupil to be more worthy of your regard than you have hitherto found him; and at all events, that he will never be otherwise than sincere and true to you.

P. B. SHELLEY.

To
  Mr. William Godwin,
                    London.

LETTER VIII.

MY DEAR SIR,

At length we are in a manner settled. The difficulty of obtaining a house in Wales (like many other difficulties) is greater than I had imagined. We determined, on quitting Dublin, to settle in Merionethshire, the scene of Fleetwood's early life, but there we could find not even temporary accommodation. We traversed the whole of North, and a part of South Wales fruitlessly, and our peregrinations have occupied nearly all the time since the date of my last.

We are no longer in Dublin. Never did I behold in any other spot a contrast so striking as that which grandeur and misery form in that unfortunate country. How forcibly do I feel the remark which you put into the mouth of Fleetwood, that the distress which in the country humanizes the heart, by its infrequency, is calculated in a city, by the multiplicity of its demands for relief, to render us callous to the contemplation of wretchedness! Surely the inequality of rank is not felt so oppressively in England! Surely something might be devised for Ireland, even consistent with the present state of politics to ameliorate its condition!

Curran at length called on me. I dined twice at his house. Curran is certainly a man of great abilities, but it appears to me that he undervalues his powers when he applies them to what is usually the subject of his conversation. I may not possess sufficient taste to relish humour, or his incessant comicality may weary that which I possess. He does not possess that mould of mind which I have been accustomed to contemplate with the highest feelings of respect and love. In short, though Curran indubitably possesses a strong understanding and a brilliant fancy, I should not have beheld him with the feelings of admiration which his first visit excited, had he not been your intimate friend.

Nantgwillt, the place where we now reside, is in the neighbourhood of scenes marked deeply on my mind by the thoughts which possessed it when present among them. The ghosts of these old friends have a dim and strange appearance, when resuscitated, in a situation so altered as mine is, since I felt that they were alive. I have never detailed to you my short, yet eventful life ; but, when we meet, if my account be not candid, sincere, and full, how

unworthy should I be of such a friend
and adviser as that whom I now
address !

We are not yet completely certain of
being able to obtain the house where
now we are.   It has a farm of two
hundred acres, and the rent is but
forty-eight pounds* per annum.   The
cheapness, beauty,   and retirement,
make this place in every point of view
desirable.   Nor can I view this scenery,
—mountains and rocks seeming to form
a barrier round this quiet valley, which
the tumult of the world may never
overleap ; the guileless habits of the
Welsh,—without associating *your* presence with the idea, that of your wife,
your children, and one other friend, to
complete the picture which my mind
has drawn to itself of felicity.   Steal,
if possible, my revered friend, one

---

* This should be "*ninety*-eight pounds " : see letters
to Medwin, Senr., in Medwin's *Life of Shelley*, vol. i.,
p. 378, &c.

summer from the cold hurry of business, and come to Wales.—Adieu.

Harriet desires to join me in kindest remembrances to yourself, Mrs. G[odwin], and family. She joins also in earnest wishes that you would all visit us.

Yours,

P. B. SHELLEY.

To
  Mr. William Godwin,
        London.

LETTER IX.

Nantgwillt, [Rhayader].
June 3rd, 1812.
[*Wednesday.*]

My Dear Sir,

I hasten to dissipate the unfavour-
able impressions you seem to have
received from my silence.   Mrs. Godwin, in a letter to my wife, mentions
the existence of *your* letter in Ireland.
This I have never been able to recover :
indeed, I am confident that the date
of your last was considerably anterior
to the 30th of March.

My health has been far from good
since I wrote to you ; and I have been
day after day tormented and rendered
anxious by the delay of legal business
necessary to secure this house to us.   I

do not say that anything can absolutely excuse any neglect to you; but the constant expectancy that the succeeding day would bring a train of thought more favourable than the present, together with your expected letter, may be permitted to palliate it.

I hope, my venerated friend, that you will soon permit the time to arrive when you may know me as I am; when you may consult those lineaments which cannot deceive; and be placed in a situation which will obviate the possibility of delusion.

I revert with pleasure to the latter part of your letter, and entreat you to erase from your mind the impressions which occasioned the former. They shall never, assure yourself, find occasion of renewal.

Until my marriage, my life had been a series of illness (as it was of a nervous and spasmodic nature) which in a degree incapacitated me for study. I nevertheless, in the intervals of comparative health, read romances, and those the most marvellous ones, unremittingly ; and pored over the reveries of Albertus Magnus and Paracelsus, the former of which I read in Latin, and probably gained more knowledge of that language from that source than from all the discipline of Eton. My fondness for natural magic and ghosts abated, as my age increased. I read Locke, Hume, Reid, and whatever metaphysics came in my way, without however renouncing poetry, an attachment to which has characterized all my wanderings and changes. I did not truly *think* and *feel*, however, until I read *Political Justice*, though my thoughts and feelings, after this period, have been more painful, anxious, and vivid,—more inclined to action and less to theory.   Before, I was republican : Athens appeared to me the model of governments.   But afterwards Athens bore in my mind the same relation to perfection that Great Britain did to Athens.

I fear that I am wanting in that mild and equable benevolence concerning which you question me. Still, I flatter myself that I improve; at all events, I have willingness, and "desire never fails to generate capacity."

My knowledge of the chivalric age is small : do not conceive that I intend it to remain so. During my existence I have incessantly speculated, thought, and read. A great deal of this labour has been uselessly directed ; still, I am willing to hope that some portion of the stores thus improvidently accumulated will turn to account. I have just finished reading *Le Système de la Nature, par M. Mirabaud.** Do you know the real author ? It appears to me a work of uncommon powers.

* Written by Baron d'Holbach. Shelley inserted a long extract from this work in the *Notes* to *Queen Mab*.

I write this to you by return of post, solicitous as quickly as possible to reassure you of my fidelity and truth. I will soon write one more at length, and with answers more satisfactory to the questions in the latter part of yours.

Believe me, with sincerest respect,

Yours most truly,

P. B. SHELLEY.

To
  Mr. William Godwin,
              London.

LETTER X.

Cwm Elan, Rhayader.
June 11th, 1812.
[*Thursday.*]

My Dear Sir,

I will no longer delay returning my grateful and cordial acknowledgments for your inestimable letter of March 30. That it is most affectionate and kind I deeply feel and thankfully confess. I can return no other answer than that I will become all that you believe and wish me to be. I should regard it as my greatest glory, should I be judged worthy to solace your declining years; it is a pleasure the realization of which I anticipate with confident hopes, and which it shall be my study to deserve. I will endeavour to subdue the impatience of my nature, so incompatible with true benevolence.

I know that general philanthropy does not permit its votaries to relax, even when hope appears to languish; or to indulge bitterness of feeling against the very worst, the most mistaken, of men.

To these faults, in a considerable degree, I plead guilty; at all events, I have now a stimulus adequate to excite me to the conquest of them.

I yet know little of the chivalric age. The ancient romances, in which are depicted the manners of those times, never fell in my way. I have read Southey's *Amadis of Gaul* and *Palmerin of England*, but at a time when I was little disposed to philosophize on the manners they describe. I have also read his *Chronicle of the Cid*. It is written in a simple and impressive style, and surprised me by the extent of accurate reading evinced by the references. But I read it hastily; and it did not please me so much as it will on a reperusal, seasoned by your authority and opinion.

It requires no great study to attain an intimate knowledge of Grecian and Roman history; it requires but common feeling to appreciate and acknowledge the resplendent virtues with which it is replete. The first doubts which arise in boyish minds concerning the genuineness of the Christian religion, as a revelation from the divinity, are often excited by a contemplation of the virtues and genius of Greece and Rome. Shall Socrates and Cicero perish, whilst the meanest hind of modern England inherits eternal life?

I mean not to affirm that this is the first argument with which I would combat the delusions of superstition; but it certainly was one of the first that operated to convince me that they were delusions.

What do you think of Eaton's trial
and sentence?   I mean not to insinu-
ate that this poor bookseller has any
characteristics in common with Socrates
or Jesus Christ.   Still, the spirit which
pillories and imprisons him is the same
which brought them to an untimely
end : still, even in this enlightened age,
the moralist and reformer may expect
coercion analogous to that used with
the humbler yet zealous imitator of
their endeavours.   I have thought of
addressing the public on the subject,
and indeed have begun an outline of
the address.*   May I be favoured with
your remarks on it before I send it to
the world ?

We are unexpectedly compelled to
quit Nantgwillt.   I hope, however,
before long time has elapsed, to find a
home.   These accidents are unavoid-

* When completed this projected "address to the
public" was issued as *A Letter to Lord Ellenborough,
occasioned by the sentence which he passed on Mr.
D. I. Eaton.*

able to a minor. I hope, wherever we are, you, Mrs. Godwin, and your children will come this summer.

I do not suppose we shall remain here longer than a week. All letters directed here will securely and certainly be forwarded. Harriet desires to join me in everything that is respectful and affectionate to yourself, Mrs. G [odwin], and family, my venerated friend.

Believe me to remain, yours most sincerely,

P. B. SHELLEY.

To
  Mr. William Godwin,
         London.

LETTER XI.

LYMOUTH, BARNSTAPLE.
July 5th, 1812.
[*Sunday.*]

MY DEAR SIR,

I write to acknowledge the pleasure I anticipate in the perusal of some letters from you and yours which have not yet reached us. The post comes to Lymouth but twice in a week; and some allowance is to be made for the casualties which attend an event by which we have been unexpectedly unsettled. We were all so much pre-possessed in favour of Mr. Eton's house that nothing but the invincible ob-jection of scarcity of room would have induced us, even after seeing it, to resign the predetermination we had formed of taking it. We now reside in a small cottage ; but the poverty and humbleness of the apartments is compensated for by their number, and we can invite our friends with a consciousness that there is enclosed space wherein they may sleep, which was not to be found at Mr. Eton's.

I will, in the absence of other topics, explain to you my reason for fixing upon this residence. I am, as you know, a minor, and as such depend upon a limited income ($£400$ per annum) allowed by my relatives. Upon this income justice and humanity have many claims, and the necessary expenses of existing in conformity to some habitudes which may be said to be interwoven with our being dissipate the remainder. I might, it is true, raise money on my prospects, but the percentage is so enormous that it is with extreme unwillingness I should have recourse to a step which I might then be induced to repeat, even to a ruinous frequency and extent. The involvement of my patrimony would interfere with schemes on which it is my fondest delight to speculate. I may truly, therefore, be classed generically with those minors who pant for twenty-one, though I trust that the specific difference is very, very wide. The expenses incurred by the failure of our attempt in settling at Nantgwillt have rendered it necessary for us to settle for a time in some cheap residence, in order to recover our pecuniary independence.

I will still hope that you and your estimable family will, before much time has elapsed, become inmates of our house. This house boasts not such accommodation as I should feel satisfied in offering you; but I propose a plan which, if it meets your approbation, may prove an interlude to our meeting, and become an earnest that much time will not elapse before its occurrence. I have a friend* . . . . But first I will make you in some measure acquainted with her. She is a woman with whom her excellent qualities made me acquainted. Though deriving her birth from a very humble source, she contracted, during youth, a very deep and refined habit of thinking. Her mind, naturally inquisitive and penetrating, overstepped the bounds of prejudice ; she formed for herself an unbeaten path of life.

By the patronage of a lady whose liberality of mind is singular, this woman, at the age of twenty was enabled to commence the conduct of a school. She concealed not the uncommon modes of thinking which she had adopted, and publicly instructed youth as a Deist and a Republican. When I first knew her, she had not read *Political Justice*, yet her life ap-

* Miss Elizabeth Hitchener.

peared to me in a great degree modelled upon its precepts. Such is the woman who is about to become an inmate of our family. She will pass through London, and I shall take the liberty of introducing to you one whom I do not consider unworthy of the advantage.

As soon as we recover our financial liberty, we mean to come to London. Why may not Fanny come to Lymouth with her and return with us all to London in the autumn? I entreat you to look with a favourable eye upon this request, and indeed our hearts long for a personal intercourse with those to whom they are devoted; yet I fear, from the tenor of Mrs. G[odwin]'s letter, that we must give up the hope of seeing you. This disappointed hope determines us to journey to London *as soon as we can.*

This place is beautiful : it equals— Harriet says it exceeds—Nantgwillt.

Mountains certainly of not less perpendicular elevation than 1000 feet are broken abruptly into valleys of indescribable fertility and grandeur. The climate is so mild that myrtles of an immense size twine up our cottage, and roses blow in the open air in winter. In addition to these is the sea, which dashes against a rocky and caverned shore, presenting an ever-changing view. All "shows of sky and earth, of sea and valley," are here.

Adieu. Believe how devotedly and sincerely I must now remain yours,

P. B. SHELLEY.

I write this letter by return of post, and send purposely to Barnstaple. I have *more* to say ; but will reserve it until I receive the letters which are on the way.

To
Mr. William Godwin,
London.

LETTER XII.

LYMOUTH, [BARNSTAPLE].
July 7th, 1812.
[*Tuesday.*]

MY DEAR SIR,

The person whom I sent yesterday
to the post-town has returned.   He
brought those letters from you and
yours, which have been forwarded from
Cwm Elan to Chepstow.   It is a
singular coincidence that in my last
letter I entered into details respecting
my mode of life, and unfolded to you
the reasons by which I was induced, on
being disappointed in Mr. Eton's house,
to seek an unexpensive retirement.   I
feel my heart throb exultingly when, as
I read the misgivings of your mind concerning my rectitude, I reflect that I
have to a certain degree refuted them by

anticipation. My letter, dated the 5th, will prove to you that it is not to live in splendour, which I hate,—*not* to accumulate indulgences, which I despise, that my present conduct was adopted. Most unworthy, indeed, should I be of that high destiny which he who is your friend and pupil must share, if I was not myself practically a proselyte to that doctrine by promulgating which with unremitting zeal and industry I have become the object of hatred and suspicion.

Our *cottage* (for such, not nominally, but really, it is) exceeds not in its accommodations the dwellings of the peasantry which surround it. Its beds are of the plainest, I may say the coarsest, materials ; and from the single consideration that accommodations for personal convenience were glaringly defective, did I refrain in my last letter from pressing the request, whose concession is nearest to my desires, that *you* would come to this lovely solitude, and bring to a conclusion that state of acquaintance which stands between us, to a *perfect* intimacy. I was beginning a sentence in the middle of the second page of my letter, in which I should have pressed you to come *here*, when Harriet interrupted me, bade me consider that your health was delicate, that our rooms were complete *servants' rooms.* I finished the sentence as it stands. She added that we would hasten our journey to London, and that *you all* should live with us. It was the thought of the moment ; I send it you without comment, as it arose. See my defence. Yet, my esteemed and venerated friend, accept my thanks ;— consider yourself as yet more beloved by me for the manner in which you have reproved my suppositionary errors ; and ever may you, like the tenderest and wisest of parents, be on the watch to detect those traits of vice which, yet undiscovered, are nevertheless marked on the tablet of my character, so that I pursue undeviatingly the . path which you first cleared through the wilderness of life.

I said, in my last letter, that there are certain habitudes in conformity to which it is almost necessary that persons who have contracted them should exist. By this I do not mean that a splendid mansion, or an equipage, is in any degree essential to life ; but that, if I was employed at the loom or the plough, and my wife in culinary business and housewifery, we should, in the present state of society, quickly become very different beings, and, I may add, less useful to our species. Nor, consistently with invincible ideas of delicacy, can two persons of opposite sexes, unconnected by certain ties, sleep in the same apartment. Probably, in a regenerated state of society, agriculture and manufacture would be compatible with the most powerful intellect, and most polished manners; probably delicacy, as it relates to sexual distinction, would disappear;—yet now, a plough-boy can with difficulty acquire refinement of intellect; and promiscuous sexual intercourse, under the present system of thinking, would inevitably lead to consequences the most injurious to the happiness of mankind. Mr. Eton's house had not sufficient bedrooms, *scarcely* sufficient for ourselves, and you and your family must sleep; for, my dear friend, believe me that I would not willingly take a house, for any time, whither you could not come. Have I written desultorily? Is my explanation of habitudes incorrect, or indistinct? Pardon me, for I am anxious to lose no time in communicating my sentiments.

Harriet is writing to Fanny *; if she

* Fanny Imlay, the daughter of Mary Wollstonecraft, and Gilbert Imlay, but frequently spoken of as "Fanny Godwin."

is particular in her invitation of Fanny, it is not meant exclusively. There are a sufficient quantity of bed-rooms ; and, if the humbleness of their quality is no objection, I need not say,—Come, thou venerated and excellent friend, and make us happy.—Adieu !

Believe me, with the utmost sincerity and truth,   Ever yours,

P. B. SHELLEY.

(Single sheet.)

To
Mr. William Godwin,
London.

LETTER XIII.

LYMOUTH, [BARNSTAPLE].
July 29th, 1812.
[*Wednesday.*] *

MY DEAR GODWIN,

I have never seen you,† and yet I think I know you; I think I knew you even before I ever heard from you, whilst yet it was a question with me whether you were living or dead. It has appeared to me that there are lineaments in the soul, as well as in the face; lineaments, too, less equivocal

---

* This letter exhibits Shelley in a peculiarly *negative* frame of mind :—the Shelley of the "Notes" to *Queen Mab.*

† On *September* 18th, 1812, William Godwin unexpectedly arrived at Lymouth—only to find, to his very considerable vexation, that the Shelleys had left since *August* 31st. [See *Shelley Memorials,* p. 41]. It was in London, and not until the following *October* (1812), that Godwin first met his future son-in-law.

and deceptive than those which result from mere physical organization. This opinion may be illusory; if I find it so, it shall be retracted.

You say three letters of yours have been unanswered. I waited to know whether those of mine contained any topics worthy of notice or discussion. I find they do not; therefore, let us pass on.

To begin with Helvétius. I have read *Le Système de la Nature*, and suspect this to be Helvétius's by your charges against it. It is a book of uncommon powers, yet too obnoxious to accusations of sensuality and selfishness. Although, like you, an irreconcileable enemy to the system of self-love, both from a feeling of its deformity and a conviction of its falsehood, I can by no means conceive how the loftiest disinterestedness is incompatible with the strictest materialism. In fact, the doctrine which affirms that there is no such thing as matter, and that which affirms that all is matter, appear to me perfectly indifferent in the question between benevolence and self-love. I cannot see how they interfere with each other, or why the two doctrines of materialism and dis-interestedness cannot be held in one mind, as independently of each other as the two truths that a cricket-ball is round and a box square. Immateriality seems to me nothing but a simple denial of the presence of matter, of the presence of all the forms of being with which our senses are acquainted ; and it surely is somewhat inconsistent to assign real existence to what is a mere negation of all that actual world to which our senses introduce us.

I have read Berkeley ; and the perusal of his arguments tended more than anything to convince me that Immater-ialism, and other words of general usage, deriving all their force from mere predicates in *non*, were invented by the pride of philosophers to conceal their ignorance, even from themselves. If I err in what I say, or if I differ from you (though in this point I think I do not), Reason stands arbiter between us. Reason, if I may be permitted to personify it, is as much your superior as you are mine. An hour and a thousand years are equally incommensurate with eternity.

With respect to Helvétius's opinion of the omnipotence of education, *there* I submit to your authority, because authority, derived from experience such as yours, is reason. I will own that the opinion of Helvétius, until very lately, has been mine.

You know that in most points I agree with you. As I see you in *Political Justice*, I agree with you. Your *Enquirer* is replete with speculations in which I sympathize ; yet the arguments there in favour of classical learning failed to

remove all my doubts on that point.
I am not sufficiently vain and dog-
matical to say that *now* I have *no*
doubts on the deleteriousness of
classical education ; but it certainly is
my opinion (nor has your last letter
sufficed to refute it) that the evils of
acquiring Greek and Latin considerably
overbalance the benefit. But why,
because I think so, should it even be
supposed necessary by you to warn
me against fearing that *you feel
displeasure?* Assure yourself that the
picture of you in the retina of my
intellect is a standing proof to me that
its original is capable of extending to
opinions the most unlimited toleration,
and that he will scan with disgust
nothing but a defect of the heart. Let
Reason, then, be arbiter between us.
Yet sometimes I am struck with dismay
when I consider that, placed where you
are, high up on the craggy mountain of
knowledge, you will scarcely condescend

to doubt, even sufficiently for the purposes of discussion, that opinion which you hold, although by that doubting you might fit me for following in your footsteps. Yet I will explain my reasons for doubting the efficacy of classical learning as a means of forwarding the interests of the human race.

In the first place, I do not perceive how one of the truths of *Political Justice* rests on the excellence of ancient literature. That Latin and Greek have contributed to form your character it were idle to dispute; but in how great a *degree* have they contributed? Are not the reasonings on which your system is founded utterly distinct from and unconnected with the excellence of Greece and Rome? Was not the government of republican Rome, and most of those of Greece, as oppressive and arbitrary as that of Great Britain is at present? And what do we learn from their poets? As you

have yourself acknowledged somewhere, " they are fit for nothing but the
perpetuation of the noxious race of
heroes in the world." Lucretius
forms, perhaps, the single exception.
Throughout the whole of their literature runs a vein of thought similar to
that which you have so justly censured
in Helvétius. Honour—and the opinion either of contemporaries, or more
frequently of posterity—is set so much
above virtue as, according to the last
words of Brutus, to make it nothing
but an empty name. Their politics
sprang from the same narrow and cor-
rupted source : witness the interminable
aggressions between each other of the
states of Greece ; the thirst of conquest
with which even republican Rome
desolated the earth. They are our
masters in politics because we are so
immoral as to prefer self-interest to
virtue, and expediency to positive good.

You say that words will neither debauch our understandings nor distort our moral feelings. You say that the time of youth could not be better employed than in the acquisition of classical learning. But *words* are the very things that so eminently contribute to the growth and establishment of prejudice : the learning of *words*, before the mind is capable of attaching correspondent ideas to them, is like possessing machinery with the use of which we are so unacquainted as to be in danger of misusing it. But words are merely signs of ideas. How many evils, and how great evils, spring from annexing inadequate and improper ideas to words ! The words honour, virtue, duty, goodness, are examples of this remark. Besides, we only want one distinct sign for one idea. Do you not think that there is much more danger of our wanting ideas for the signs of them already made, than of our wanting these signs for inexpressible ideas? I should think that natural philosophy, medecine, astronomy, and, above all, history, could be sufficient employments for immaturity; employments which would completely fill up the era of tutelage, and render unnecessary all expedients for losing time well, by gaining it safely.

Of the Latin language, as a grammar. I think highly. It is a key to the European languages, and we can hardly be said to know our own without first attaining a complete knowledge of it. Still, I cannot help considering it as an affair of minor importance, inasmuch as the science of things is superior to the science of words. Nor can I help considering the vindicators of ancient learning—I except you, not from politeness, but because you, unlike them, are willing to subject your opinions to reason—as the vindicators of a literary despotism ; as the tracers of a circle which is intended to shut out from real knowledge (and to which this fictitious knowledge is attached) all who do not breathe the air of prejudice, or who will not support the established systems of politics, religion, and morals. I have as great a contempt for Cobbett as you can have ; but it is because he is a dastard and a time-server,—he has no humanity, no refinement. But, were he a classical scholar, would he have more? Did Greek and Roman literature refine the soul of Johnson? Does it extend the views of the thousand narrow bigots educated in the very bosom of classicality? But

" In publica commoda peccem
" Si longo sermone morer tua tempora," *

says Horace at the commencement of his longest letter.

Well, adieu. All join in kindest

* Shelley seems to have been fond of this quotation. It had already appeared in his letter to Godwin dated *January* 16*th*, 1812 [see *ante.* p. 17]. It also reappears in one of his letters to Peacock.

love to your amiable family, of whom I have forgotten to speak, but not to think; and I remain

Very truly and affectionately yours,

P. B. SHELLEY.

To
   Mr. W. Godwin,
         London.

LETTER XIV.

BISHOPGATE,
January 7th, 1815 [1816.]
[*Saturday.*]

SIR,

I will endeavour to give you as clear as possible a history of the proceedings between myself and my father.

A small portion of the estates to which I am entitled in reversion, were comprehended in the will of Mr. John Shelley, my great uncle, and devised to the same uses as the larger portion which was settled by my father's marriage, jointly by my grandfather and father. This portion was valued at £18,000, which my father purchased of me with an equivalent of £11,000.

VOL. I.   B B

I signed on this occasion two deeds, the one was to empower my attorney to suffer what is called a recovery, the other a counterpart of the deed of conveyance.

Before these transactions, however, and at the very commencement of our negotiations, I signed a deed which was the preliminary and the basis of the whole business. My grandfather had left me the option of receiving a life estate in some very large sum (I think £140,000) on condition that I would prolong the entail, so as to possess only a life estate in my original patrimony. These conditions I never intended to accept, although Longdill considered them very favourable to me, and urged me by all means to grasp at the offer. It was my father's interest and wish that I should refuse these conditions, because my younger brother would inherit, in default of my compliance with them, this life-estate.

Longdill and Whitton * therefore made
an agreement that I should resign my
rights to this property, and that my
father, in exchange for the concession,
should give me the full price for my
reversion. In compliance with the
terms of this agreement, I signed a
deed importing that I disclaimed my
grandfather's property. My father did
not sign his part of the agreement
because he could not do so without
forfeiting the new entail (which says
that whoever in whatever manner
endeavours to break through the intentions of the testator shall not enjoy
the fortune). But Mr. Whitton engaged tacitly to Longdill that my father
would buy the reversion on the terms
already settled.

Now, Whitton professes my father's
willingness to proceed, but urges every
consideration calculated to delay the

* Longdill was Shelley's solicitor; Whitton was
Sir Timothy's solicitor.

progress of the affair. Longdill told me that he saw Whitton wished to procure as much delay as possible, but that he still thought it was their intention not entirely to give up the negotiation. Whether both Whitton and Longdill are not quietly making their advantage out of the inexperience and credulity of myself and my father, is a doubt that has crossed my mind.

You say that you will receive no more than £1,250 for the payment of those incumbrances from which you think I may be considered as *specially* bound to relieve you. I would not desire to persuade you to sell the approbation of your friends for the difference between this sum and that which your necessities actually require. But the mention of your friends has suggested a plan to my mind which possibly you may be able to execute. You have undoubtedly some well-wishers, who, although they would refuse to give you so large a sum as £1,200, might not refuse to lend it you on security which they might consider unexceptionable. I think you could lay before any rich friend such a statement of your case as that, if he could refuse to lend £1,200 on my security, his desire of benefiting you must be exceedingly slight.

There is every probability in favour of the arrangement with my father being completed within the year. I can give evidence of the existence of negotiations between us.

If this prospect should fail, I still remain heir to property of £6,000 or £7,000 a year. Why not ask Grattan, or Mackintosh, or Lord Holland, whom I have heard named as your . . . . . .

[*The remainder of this letter is missing.*]

LETTER XV.

BISHOPGATE,
Jan[*uary*] 18*th*, 1816.
[*Wednesday.*]

SIR,

I consent to sell an annuity which shall produce enough to cover Hogan's demand, on these conditions :—

That you should agree to pay the interest until I am able to discharge the principal. I shall take your word for the fulfilment of this part of the contract.

That entire secrecy should be observed. It will be necessary that the solicitor who engages in the management of the affair should defer registering the annuity for judgment for the period of a year.

Do you know the quarter whence

the money can be produced ? I would prefer any other than Hayward, for reasons which I could enumerate if it were necessary.

The person who proposed to lend £1,000, would probably lend a quarter of that sum. You had better apply to him in the first instance and enquire whether he will do so. I, not residing in London, am obviously incompetent to conduct the affair.

Clairmont informs me that in a former instance he explained with you on the subject of the claim which you urge, to be repaid the £200 subtracted by me from the £1,200 of nominal debt which he agreed to state on your part, for the purpose of putting me in possession of the £200. He told you that he believed you to be mistaken in your construction of my message, and on explaining with me, I confirmed his remembrance of the real state of the arrangement.

Perhaps it is well that you should be informed that I consider your last letter to be written in a certain style of haughtiness and encroachment, which neither awes nor imposes on me. But I have no desire to transgress the limits which you placed to our intercourse, nor in any future instance will I make any remarks but such as arise from the strict question in discussion.

Perhaps you do well to consider every word irrelevant to that question which does not regard your personal advantage.

P. B. SHELLEY.

I forgot to inform you that no paper has been signed by my father which regards the affair of the estate. The general intention and fundamental basis of the business have been stated and admitted in many instances by Whitton in writing, though I should

conceive not in a manner which con-
stitutes a legal obligation.

[*Addressed outside.*]
   W. Godwin, Esq.,
      41, Skinner Street,
         Snow Hill,
            London.

LETTER XVI.

BISHOPGATE,
January 21*st,* 1816.
[*Saturday.*]

SIR,

It is impossible to procure any letter from Whitton, or any evidence of the affair with my father. Any attempt to possess myself of such a document would risk an entire destruction of my prospects in that quarter. But I apprehend that a reference to my banker would answer the same end. It would prove to the inquirer that I am in the regular receipt of £800 per annum. I should conceive that a person who had an opportunity of making 15 per cent. of so small a sum as £200 or £300 would consider this fact a sufficient assurance of the safety of his loan.

Particularly when he reflects in addition upon the strong presumption which he can deduce from various circumstances of the approaching settlement of my affairs.

If the person who applied to you is, contrary to my expectation, disposed to think differently of the matter, then let Hayward be applied to.

There are some objections to Hayward, some of which incite me to require caution in treating with him, some demand explanation, and are only worth considering as they impede the loan.

1st. Secrecy is to be secured which is somewhat difficult, unless his own interest is implicated.

2nd. This real or pretended want of confidence in my representations is to be overcome.

When I applied to him for the purpose of borrowing money for my own wants he inquired whether by the late arrangement with my father all incumbrances on the estate were cancelled. I replied in the affirmative since, although I did not know that Nash had been actually paid, yet an offer being then pending by which he was to receive £4,500 for what he purchased from me the year before at £2,600, I did not doubt, nor did Longdill doubt, but that he would resign on these terms his claim on the estate.

I spoke therefore according to my belief, according to the real fact, and according to the purpose for which alone it imported him to know when I replied that the estate was no longer incumbered. But indeed I know not whether Hayward would presume to make this accusation to any one, whom he knew had direct communication with me, or concerning whom it might not reasonably be doubted whether the misrepresentations did not as probably originate with any informer or with himself. Hayward is to be applied to, if your person fails. But I hope the necessity will not arise. If you clearly perceive that there is no other mode of raising the money, I do not require a day's delay. You can either apply to Hayward, or I will write to him, as you choose.

If Hayward refuses and we can raise money on my security in no manner, did it never suggest itself to you, that your signature joined with mine might effect what neither would effect singly?

With respect to the question which you ask on the subject of the £200, I certainly never gave Clairmont the smallest ground for the representation on which your mistake rests. I accept, and thank you for your explanation. If you really think me vicious, such haughtiness as I imputed to you is perhaps to be excused. But I, who do not agree with you in that opinion, cannot be expected to endure it without remonstrance. I can easily imagine how difficult it must be, in addressing a person whom we despise or dislike, to abstain from phrases, the tenor of which is peculiar to the sentiments with which we cannot help regarding such a person. Perhaps I did wrong to feel so deeply or notice so readily a spirit of which you seem so unconscious.

P. B. SHELLEY.

[*Addressed outside.*]
W. Godwin, Esq.,
41, *Skinner Street,*
Snow Hill,
London.

LETTER XVII.

BISHOPGATE,
January 23rd, 1816.
[*Monday.*]

SIR,

I fear that it is quite impossible to procure any documents from Longdill. I do not mean to say that if the loan cannot be procured without it, I will refuse to attempt to procure them. But Longdill is now out of town, and the few days that will pass during his absence may be employed in discovering whether we can do without him.

Hayward, it seems, must be applied to. Let this be done without delay. I should conceive that the same advantages which made it appear probable that the person you mentioned would find the money, would operate with greater force on Hayward.

I told Hayward that I did not know when the affair with my father would terminate, or even whether it might not be entirely abandoned.

I conceive that he relied in reality far more on my present income than my future expectations, and that if he declines to advance any additional loan, it will spring not from any doubt of the validity of my security, but because some object which he might have contemplated in his former services was not obtained.

As soon as we have procured Hayward's answer, we shall either be certain that he will advance the money, or that he will not.

If he decides in the negative, I will lose no time in taking whatever measures may appear good to you for procuring it from some other quarter.

I am most undoubtedly in earnest, as

much so as I should have been last November, had such an explanation been made as I have since received, and the same spirit of promptitude shown to share with me the burthens incident to the pecuniary difficulties with which I have been so long surrounded.

I hope that you will not refrain from applying to Hayward on the ground that these letters from Whitton may possibly be procured. · I have not myself even seen them that I recollect; and it is most likely that they would be found to express only a general intention on my father's part to divide the estates, a fact of which Hayward certainly entertains no doubt. I am indeed earnest that you should not defer to put the question to Hayward.

I am sorry that I cannot appeal to my memory for the precise words of the message which you received with the £1,000 in the spring. I am certain only that it was not, because I am aware of arrangements made in my own mind, by which it could not be, such as you represent Clairmont to have delivered it. My meaning was that you should receive no more than that £1,000 until the second settlement with my father which was then expected in November. I consider that giving in your debt at £1,200, as an accommodation to me, enabling me to procure as I did £200 which I should not otherwise have received. My message certainly in some manner expressed this view of the subject to Clairmont, and no other.

P. B. SHELLEY.

[*Addressed outside*].

W. Godwin, Esq.,

41, *Skinner Street,*

Snow Hill,

London.

Privately Printed: 1891.

www.ingramcontent.com/pod-product-compliance
Lightning Source LLC
Chambersburg PA
CBHW032019010726
47493CB00007B/2480